Puffin Books

Playtime Stories

Anyone with small children knows their insatiable interest in other children's lives, not just their big adventures but the games they play, the toys they have, and all sorts of little details about their families.

The stories in this book are just the thing to satisfy this curiosity and to stimulate it still more, with their nice homely accounts of little children helping their father to decorate a room or build a sandpit, having a 'seaside holiday' at home in the garden when the weather is hot or mislaying the money that is put out to pay the milkman.

All the children in these stories are so true to life that they seem like real playmates, because the author really does understand children, both as the mother of five and as a former Vice-Chairman of the Pre-School Playgroups Association's National Executive Committee.

Joyce Donoghue

Playtime
Stories

Illustrated by
Prudence Seward

Puffin Books

Puffin Books, Penguin Books Ltd, 27 Wrights Lane, London w8 5tz (Publishing and Editorial)
and Harmondsworth, Middlesex, England Distribution and Warehouse
Viking Penguin Inc., 40 West 23rd Street, New York, New York 10010, U.S.A.
Penguin Books Australia Ltd, Ringwood, Victoria, Australia
Penguin Books Canada Ltd, 2801 John Street, Markham, Ontario, Canada l3r 1b4
Penguin Books N.Z. Ltd, 182–190 Wairau Road, Auckland 10, New Zealand

First published 1974
Reprinted 1974, 1976, 1981, 1987, 1988

Made and printed in Great Britain by
Richard Clay Ltd, Bungay, Suffolk
Set in Monotype Baskerville

A THANK YOU TO
my children Janet, Christine,
Michael, Geoffrey and Neil,
who showed me what childhood is about
and
my friends of
the Pre-School Playgroups Association
who encouraged me to write these stories
and tried them out.
These stories are for you; thank you.

Contents

Introduction

About stories in general, and these stories in particular . . .

All children delight in stories; there is no substitute for being close to mother or father for that eagerly anticipated time 'after the baby's been fed' or 'before we put out the light and you go to sleep'.

One of the best reasons for reading or telling stories to young children is that when mother or father settles by the fire or at the bedside, he or she is really saying, 'Here I am, giving you my undivided attention. I love you and this is my way of showing you that I do.'

Reader and read-to both see the characters of the story in their mind's eye. They watch together as the story unfolds. Afterwards, perhaps they talk about it. They may wonder what happens next or make up another story. They share past and future events together in story form, and establish the relationship that will make it easy to talk together about other, more important, issues in the future.

These particular stories are about ordinary children doing ordinary things in ordinary families, because children enjoy hearing about nearly familiar things happening to other children. It's reassuring and it helps them to understand what happens to them and around them.

Some of these stories introduce situations that may worry a young child, such as mother in hospital, a new baby, being ill, a precious toy broken. They provide an opportunity for children to 'try on' their anxieties and hear of a happy outcome before something like it happens in their own lives. We meet different sizes of family: sometimes the child-in-the-story is the only child; sometimes he has a baby sister or a big brother, sometimes both. Such situations widen the child's known world. When the child-in-the-story has his particular adventure or experience, the child-being-read-to shares it imaginatively as a second-hand experience which joins the other real and second-hand experiences which he stores unconsciously at the back of his mind and uses to make sense of things and people.

The older generation is brought into some of the stories and mentioned in others. This gives added security and provides another understanding adult with a different role from that of either parent. It also helps the child to begin to form some concept of time and family relationships.

As for reading the stories, only you, the reader, know the length of story that suits your child. Indeed, what may be right for him today may be too long or too short tomorrow – and the wrong story in any case. Most of these stories can easily be split into instalments if necessary. Just look for the natural break and say something like, 'Now I wonder what happened after that? Do you think David's bricks came the next day? We'll read some more tomorrow and find out ...' And when you pick up where you left off, you can say something like, 'Now what was David doing when we stopped yesterday? Had the coalman come? . . . Do you remember the coalman? What did he do? . . .' so that the scene is set again for David's world.

These stories were also written with the reading adult in mind in that they show children behaving normally and naturally and indicate how parents can make the most of each experience. Living with children is a challenge; we so often forget how much children don't know, and find it difficult to see things their way. I hope you and your children enjoy reading *Playtime Stories*. They have been taken from real family experiences, and although friends have tried them out with groups of children, they're really meant for mothers – and fathers or grandparents – and children at home.

JOYCE DONOGHUE

1. David's Sandpit

1 The Big Dig

David's Daddy had promised to build a sandpit in the garden. One Saturday he took David into the town to see the man at the Builder's Yard and ordered a lot of bricks.

David was disappointed, and when they were going home he was very quiet.

'What's the matter, David?' asked Daddy.

'I thought we were going to get some sand,' said David.

Daddy laughed. 'I've got to make the sandpit first,' he said. 'The bricks are for the bottom of the pit. First, I must dig out the hole and then I have to lay the bricks – and you can help me.'

So, after dinner, Daddy put on his old garden shoes and David put on his boots and they went into the garden shed to fetch their spades.

'Where shall we have it?' asked Daddy, looking at the garden. 'I think it had better be by the path so you can use it when the grass is wet and I don't think we should have it too near the house. I know, we'll have it there,' and Daddy pointed to a place by the path where there was an empty bed of earth. 'I was going to put my lettuces there but they can go somewhere else . . .'

Daddy walked down the garden path with David behind him and looked at the bed. David looked at it too.

'When we've dug the soil out, we will have to put it somewhere else,' said Daddy, 'so we will need the wheelbarrow.'

Daddy fetched the barrow. He began to

dig a big hole for the sandpit with his garden spade. As he dug each spadeful of soil he threw it up into the wheelbarrow. David watched for a few minutes, then he began to dig with his little spade. He lifted a big lump of soil with it and carefully carried it over to the wheelbarrow. He patted it down with the rest and went back for some more, but after he had brought a few spadefuls to the barrow, Daddy said:

'Why don't you look for your own little barrow? I have to wait for you to put your spadefuls in before I can throw mine, and that's slowing us down.'

So David found his own little barrow in the shed and wheeled it down the path and put it next to Daddy's big one. He began to dig again. Suddenly Daddy stopped.

'Look what I've found!' he said. It was a tractor that David had lost weeks ago

when he had been playing in the garden.
'Buried treasure,' he said. 'It *is* muddy.
You had better put it in a safe place and
we can clean it later.'

So David ran up the garden path and
put his tractor next to the doorstep.

They went on digging.

'My, it is hot,' said Daddy suddenly. He
pulled off his jersey and threw it on to the
grass. David pulled off *his* jersey and put it
on top of Daddy's and they began to dig
again.

'My barrow's full,' announced David.

'And mine is quite full enough for one
load,' said Daddy, 'so let's wheel them to
that bit of garden over there, where I'm
going to grow the marrows. We can pile
it up there for now.'

They wheeled their barrows over to the
place where the marrows were to grow.
Daddy tipped up his big heavy barrow

and David tipped up his little light one. Daddy's great big load and David's little tiny load both tumbled out into a pile.

Then back they went to the sandpit hole and dug again. They dug and wheeled and tipped all afternoon till Mummy called them for tea and after tea they went back and looked at what they had done.

'It's big enough now,' said Daddy. 'It's wide enough and long enough and deep enough; I've only got to level it out and square it up and we're ready. Let's clean up the spades and your tractor. You can find your little bucket,' said Daddy, and when David came back, Daddy tipped water into it from a watering can.

'Now you'll want a nail brush,' he said, and David asked Mummy for an old one from the kitchen.

Daddy dipped his big spade into the bucket. He scrubbed the mud off with a big scrubbing brush till the steel blade shone like silver. David did the same with his little spade and the nail brush till all the mud had gone and the blade was shiny red once more. Then he scrubbed his tractor till all the mud was gone and the paint looked bright yellow again.

Next day, Daddy cut four pieces of wood, found a ball of string and went down the garden again with his spade.

'Shall I get mine?' called David.

'Not today,' said Daddy. 'I have to make the sides of the pit all even, ready for the bricks.'

He pushed a stick into one of the corners of the pit they had dug and tied the end of the string to it. Then he pushed another stick into the opposite corner and undid the ball of string till it reached from the first stick to the second one and wound it round the stick so that the string between the sticks was taut and in a straight line.

'Now I'll level off the edges of the pit till they are as straight as my line,' explained Daddy, and he took his spade and sliced off the sides till they were level with his line of string.

He did the same thing with the second

and third sides and David helped him with the fourth one. Then Daddy looked at the bottom of his pit.

'Not good enough yet,' he said and began to make the surface even by slicing off big flat slabs of soil with his spade. 'Now we'll check,' he said, and out of his pocket he brought a piece of wood about as thick as a matchbox and as long as four matchboxes and put it on the ground at the bottom of the pit.

'Come and look, David,' he said. David climbed into the pit and looked.

'Do you see this little bubble?' asked Daddy. David looked at the piece of wood and there was a little green window in the middle of it. Under the window there was a bubble. 'This is called a spirit-level,' said Daddy. 'When the ground is quite level, the bubble of air floats right to the middle of the window' – and he tipped the piece of wood a bit till the bubble ran off to one end of its window, then he tipped it the other way so that the bubble ran to the other end. Then he put it down flat again and the bubble settled down in the middle.

'That's all right then,' said Daddy. 'Now we can clean our boots and spades and as soon as the bricks come we'll finish the pit in no time. Then you can have your sand.'

2 *The Long Week*

It was Monday and Daddy went to work and David went to his Playgroup. After dinner, David looked at the pit he and Daddy had made at the week-end and wished the bricks had come. They hadn't come by tea-time, and when he looked out of the front window to see if a lorry was anywhere to be seen, there was an ice-cream van and a telephone van in the road

– but no Builder's lorry. The bricks didn't
come on Monday.

On Tuesday, Daddy went to work and
David went to Playgroup again, and when
he came home he went down to look at the
pit and he wished the bricks would hurry
up and come. Mummy called him in for
dinner, and after dinner he looked out of

the window again. There was a green-grocer's van and a TV repair van in the road, but no Builder's lorry. David and Mummy went shopping, and the bricks didn't come on Tuesday.

On Wednesday Daddy went to work. David didn't go to Playgroup on Wednes-days, and this Wednesday he went with Mummy to see his Aunty on the other side of town.

'Will they leave the bricks if we aren't at home?' he asked. Mummy was sure they would, but when she and David came home no bricks were there and the bricks didn't come on Wednesday.

On Thursday, Daddy went to work and David went to Playgroup again and when he came home he went to look at the pit and he did wish the bricks would come soon. While he was standing and wishing, he heard a noisy lorry coming up the road.

He ran indoors and just as he reached the kitchen he heard the front door bell, 'Ding dong!' He rushed to the door with Mummy. Surely it was the bricks, but: 'Five sacks of coal, Missus,' – it was the coal lorry.

David liked the coal man usually, but today he said, 'Oh, I thought you were the man with my bricks.'

'Are you expecting some bricks, son?' asked the coalman.

'Yes,' said David. 'Real house bricks to make my sandpit.'

'That's great,' said the coalman. 'Somebody's Daddy is going to be busy.'

'I wish they'd come soon,' said David.

'Perhaps they'll come tomorrow,' said the coalman kindly. 'Are you coming to help count my bags for me as usual?'

David went up the front path and sat on the wall. The coalman undid the back of his lorry and let it fall with a bang. Then he turned his back to it and reaching up over his head he took hold of the first bag with his hands. Carefully taking the weight on to his back he walked steadily down the path, round the side of the house and through the side gate to the coal bunker where Mummy had opened the lid. David followed. The coalman tipped the coal out of the sack and it tumbled into the coal bunker, 'rumble, rumble, rumble!' and a cloud of black dust rose out of the open lid. David followed the coalman back up the path. 'One,' said the coalman and threw the sack on the path by his lorry.

'One,' said David. The coalman took the second sack down to the bunker and brought it back empty.

'Two,' said the coalman.

'Two,' said David.

David watched him heave the third

heavy sack of coal off the lorry and followed him down the path and back.

'Three,' said the coalman, and 'Three,' said David.

The coalman took out a grimy handkerchief from his pocket and wiped his face. He was hot. 'Two more,' he said. He loaded himself with the fourth sack and soon he was back again.

'Four,' he said, 'and now for the last one.'

David watched as he hauled the full bag off the lorry, heard the coal rumble into the bunker and waited for him to come back. He didn't come so David went down the path to see what had happened. Mummy was signing a piece of paper for the coalman and he was holding the fifth sack in his hand.

'Good morning,' said the coalman and walked up the path for the last time. He threw the sack on top of the others.

'Five,' he said.

'Five,' said David, and the coalman picked the sacks up one at a time and threw them into the back of his lorry.

'One, two, three, four, five,' shouted the coalman and David together.

The coalman hitched up the back of his lorry, said good-bye to David, climbed into his cab and drove away. David went back down the path and shut the side gate. Mummy was sweeping up the black dust round the coal bunker.

The bricks didn't come on Thursday.

On Friday, Daddy went to work and David went to Playgroup again and – what do you think? When Mummy and he walked together up the road on their way home there was a pile of bricks outside the front gate. David *was* excited. 'They've come, they've come!' he shouted. 'Lots and lots of them.'

'Too many for you to count,' laughed
Mummy. The bricks were in a tidy pile
side by side and on top of each other. The
lorry man had had a wonderful time making a great castle of bricks.

David rubbed one with his finger; it felt rough and when he looked he saw there were little holes all over it. He picked up one of the bricks to put it in a different place. It was heavy, much heavier than the wooden blocks at Playgroup, and he needed both hands.

'After dinner', said Mummy, 'we'll begin to take them into the back garden. We can't leave this huge pile of bricks on the path in everybody's way.'

David patted the brick he had just put down and ran indoors after Mummy. There was a smile all over his face. The bricks had come! They would have a busy afternoon with the bricks and tomorrow Daddy and he would soon make the pit ready for the sand.

'Bricks and sand, bricks and sand!' David sang as he washed his hands.

Friday was a lovely day.

3 'Bricks and Sand!'

You remember David, don't you? He was the boy who was going to have his very own sandpit in the garden. Do you remember how he helped Daddy to dig the hole for it and how they made it all smooth and level inside ready for the bricks which were to line it – and how David waited and waited for those bricks to come so that Daddy could finish the pit. He had to wait on Monday, and Tuesday, and Wednesday and Thursday . . .

And at last the bricks had come – David and Mummy had found them in a tidy pile outside the gate when they came home from Playgroup on Friday dinner-time.

After dinner, Mummy fetched the big barrow and David fetched the little one. Mummy loaded up her big one with twenty bricks and David loaded up his little one with four, and they wheeled their barrows down the path, through the side gate and down the back path, where they carefully unloaded their bricks one by one ready for Daddy to start laying the base of the sandpit on Saturday.

Up the garden they went and out in front to fill their barrows, and then back down the garden again. The pile at the front gate was getting smaller and smaller and the pile by the pit was getting bigger and bigger. David's legs and his back were getting tired and so were Mummy's.

'Let's have a break,' said Mummy. They left the bricks and went indoors to make a pot of tea for Mummy and a glass of squash for David.

'Oh my goodness!' said Mummy. 'It's time I started cooking the meal. Daddy can finish off when he comes home, it won't take long now.'

Daddy came home late on Friday nights, so David went to bed before he came in. He was worried about the bricks. 'Will it be dark when Daddy comes home? Will he be able to move the bricks in the dark?'

'No, it won't be dark, and it won't take him long,' said Mummy, and she kissed David and drew the curtains. 'Tomorrow is Saturday,' she added. 'Daddy will have all day to brick the sandpit. It will soon be finished now.'

'Sand and bricks . . . sand and bricks,' hummed David sleepily.

On Saturday morning when David woke up he ran into Mummy's and Daddy's room and looked through the window. The bricks had gone from the front gate. 'Come on,' he shouted. 'It's sunny and the bricks are ready. We can finish the pit.'

After breakfast, Daddy put on his old garden shoes, and David put on his boots.

Daddy put his spirit-level in his trouser pocket.

They walked down the garden and Daddy stood in the pit he had made last week-end and picked up the first brick. Carefully he laid it in the corner of the pit and put his spirit-level on top to see if it was level. He pushed the brick down into the damp earth. David picked up the next brick and handed it to Daddy . . . Soon there was a row of bricks all along the edge. They laid another row and another . . . Mummy brought a

tray of drinks down to them and they stopped and looked at their work. It was like a house wall, only it was flat on the bottom of the pit.

By dinner time, the last corner was filled. David was excited: the pit was nearly finished. 'Bricks and sand, sand and bricks,' he sang as he ran up the garden path.

But there were still some bricks over. Daddy explained that these were to make a strong wall all the way round and after dinner David helped him make some cement in a bucket. Daddy built a little wall all round the inside of the pit and fixed each brick with the cement. And still there were some bricks left over. 'These are for the top, to make a proper edge for you to sit on,' said Daddy. 'I'll finish it on Sunday.'

And he did. At twelve o'clock the pit was finished. 'All we want now is the sand,' said Mummy admiring the work.

'Not quite,' said Daddy. 'I must make a cover to put over the sandpit at night, or when it's raining. We can't have nextdoor's cat digging in it, can we? And we don't want the sand turned into a mud pie if it rains too hard.'

After dinner, Daddy made a frame with six laths of wood, four round the edge and two across the middle like a big 'X' to stop it bending. He cut out a large sheet of polythene to fit on to the frame and fixed it first with some sticky tape. Then he fixed some chicken wire over the top of the polythene and tacked it down with double nails called staples. David helped him hammer them in.

'Sand and bricks, bricks and sand,' sang David, as he hammered.

'And now we are ready,' said Daddy. 'The sand will come tomorrow and I shall be at home in the afternoon to move it.'

When David came home from Playgroup on Monday, the sand had not
come. He was worried. 'But Daddy said
he was coming home early to move it,' he
said.

Just then, a lorry turned into the road
and drove slowly down. The driver was
looking at all the numbers to see which
house he had to go to.

'Number 12?' he shouted.

'That's right,' Mummy called back.

'A yard of washed sea sand,' the driver
announced and jumped out of his cab.
David watched as he undid the back and
climbed up into his lorry. With a shovel he
pushed the golden sand off the back and
into a pile on the path. It was soon done
and the sand looked like a sand castle at the
seaside, big at the bottom and tapering off
to a point at the top.

'One lucky boy,' said the lorry driver as

Mummy signed his piece of paper, and he had just gone when Daddy walked up.

You can guess what Daddy and David did that afternoon, can't you? Yes, they shovelled the sand into their barrows and wheeled it down to the pit and threw it in, and soon the bricks at the bottom were all hidden and the sand came half way up the side walls. And then it nearly reached the top.

'Last load,' said Daddy as he swept the path clean and David wheeled his little barrow down the path for the

last time and tipped it into the sand in the pit.

It was lovely. There was a square of smooth soft sand. David knelt on the edging bricks and put his hand deep into the sand and brought out two big handfuls. Slowly he let the sand trickle through his fingers to make a little pile. He was so happy he was laughing out loud.

'Look Daddy!' he shouted, turning round.

'Click!' Mummy was there with a camera and she had taken a picture of David calling Daddy to look at the sand.

'What a happy face,' she laughed. 'We'll have a picture of your first time in the sandpit and I expect Grandma would like one too.'

David ran up the path to fetch his tipper lorry and a scoop and there wasn't a happier

boy anywhere that Monday afternoon than
David in his new sandpit.

'Bricks and sand; sand and bricks,' he
sang to himself as he played in the sandpit
that he and Daddy had made together.

2. Michael's Boat

Michael lived in a house near the park. He had a brother called Jonathan, a big boy who went to school, and he had a baby sister who wasn't big enough to walk yet.

There were two things Michael liked doing best of all. One was to go with Jonathan to the pond in the park and help him sail his boat, and the other was to help Daddy with his hammering and nailing.

But when Daddy was at work, and Jonathan was at school, he couldn't go to the park and sail the boat, and he couldn't use Daddy's big hammer because he might hurt himself if there was no one to help him.

So Michael would sigh, '*When* will it be Saturday, so I can help Jonathan sail his boat?' And, '*When* will it be Saturday, so I can help Daddy make his shelves?'

And his mother would say, 'Not today, and not tomorrow, but the day after will be Saturday.'

Sometimes, they would go to the park with baby Jane in the pram, and Michael would play with other boys, but he still longed for Saturday to come.

One day, Grandfather came to stay, and Michael told him about sailing the boat on the pond, and about making shelves with Daddy.

Next morning, Grandfather went to the shops very early, while Mummy and Michael were busy bathing baby Jane. When he came back, he said, 'Michael, I have a surprise for you.'

What do you think Grandfather had bought for Michael? No, not a boat so he could sail it on his own in the park. He wasn't big enough to go there on his own. But – Yes! Grandfather had bought a small hammer!

'See, Michael,' said Grandfather, 'I've bought you a hammer for your very own. It's not too heavy for you, and you can learn to use it properly. And here is your very own box of nails, and here is a bag of wood. What will you make with them?'

'A boat,' said Michael, 'that's what I'll make.'

So Michael chose a long piece of wood for his boat, and his mother found an old tray which Michael could use as a work bench, and while Jane sat outside in the pram, Michael banged and banged with his hammer and nails. There were nails in the front and nails in the back, and nails all along the middle.

'These are the funnels, and these are the masts, and these are the railings to stop

people falling into the water,' explained Michael.

After dinner, Grandfather said, 'Let's go and sail your boat.' But he didn't take Michael to the pond in the park. He took him down to the bus stop at the end of the road.

'Where are we going?' asked Michael.

'Your boat hasn't got sails, so the wind can't blow it along. And it hasn't got a motor, so it can't go on its own,' said Grandfather. 'We must find some water that will make it move.'

Then the bus came along, and Grandfather and Michael paid their fares. Michael held his boat on his lap and watched the houses going by. Soon it was time to get off. There was a bridge over some water and a path close by. It was a river, not a big river with real boats on it, just a little river, and the water was moving under the bridge.

'This is the water for your boat,' said Grandfather, and they walked down to the path as near as they could to the river. 'Now we'll launch your boat,' he said, 'but we can't get right down to the water, so we must throw it in.'

Michael threw his boat into the middle of the river. Splash! Down it went under the water, then up it bobbed again. The water was moving quite fast in the middle. Michael's boat suddenly turned round till it faced the way the water was going, and then it began to move.

'Look!' shouted Michael. 'My boat is sailing. It's going to America! Good-bye boat!' Grandfather and Michael walked slowly along the path and Michael's boat floated along in the river beside them. The boat went under a bridge, and Michael ran ahead to watch it come out the other side. They walked and walked, and Grandfather said, 'At the next bridge we'll go up and watch your boat sail away down the river to the sea.'

So when they reached the next bridge, Michael and Grandfather went and stood by the railings and watched the boat sail away down the river. They watched until they couldn't see it any more.

'It will reach the sea by tea time,' said Michael. 'Tomorrow, I'll make another boat.'

Then Grandfather and Michael found

the bus stop and went home for tea. Mother said, 'How did your boat sail?'

'The river made it sail,' said Michael. 'It's sailing all the way to the sea. I will make another boat tomorrow.'

Note: The best tools for a small child are not a 'carpentry set' as found in many toy shops, but small real tools bought at a chain store or ironmonger's, and intended for use about the home. A small tack-hammer with 1lb. of assorted nails (1″, 2″, 4″ in length) and a box to keep them in will make an excellent start, and to them can be added a screwdriver, saw, claw-hammer, straight edge, set-square, even a vice and rasp as interest grows.

Soft wood offcuts are ideal for small children, who can't hammer nails into hard wood Pieces of cork, cotton reels etc. are interesting too.

3. Sarah's Washing Day

Sarah had a mother and a father and a baby sister called Carol, and she had three dolls: Annie, Minnie and Becky.

Annie and Minnie were made of plastic and Sarah could bath them every day, but Becky was made of cloth and couldn't be bathed or undressed. She was what Mother called a rag doll, and Grannie had brought her for Sarah when she came to stay. Although Becky couldn't be bathed, Sarah liked her best of all, and she took her to bed with her every night.

Every morning Mother would bath Sarah's baby sister Carol, in her own small bath, and Sarah would hold the safety pins and help with the baby powder. Then, while Mother fed Carol, Sarah would

bath Annie and Minnie in the baby's bath.

When Carol had finished her breakfast and been tucked into her pram for a sleep Mother and Sarah would have a drink of fruit juice together, and after that Mother would do the washing while Sarah dressed Annie and Minnie and put them in the dolls' pram with Becky, who hadn't been washed or dressed.

One sunny day, Mother said, 'It's time I washed the blankets,' and she was very busy in the sink and with the washing machine. Sarah watched Mother push the blankets into the soapy suds and squeeze them. She put her hand in the sink and brought out a pile of soapy bubbles. They were white and frothy and shone in the sunlight.

'Would you like to wash your dolls' blankets?' asked Mother. 'You go and get them out of the dolls' pram and I'll give you a bucket of warm water and soap suds.'

Sarah ran into the hall and took Annie, Minnie and Becky out of their pram. She laid them on the sofa. 'Sorry, dolls,' she said. 'It's a sunny day and I'm going to wash your blankets.'

Then back she ran to the kitchen, and almost before Mother could wrap an apron round her, Sarah put the dolls' blankets into the bucket and pushed them down into the sudsy water. She squeezed. The blankets felt smooth and slippery in the water, and Sarah rubbed and squeezed and squeezed and rubbed till they were all quite clean. Then she lifted them out and put them in another bowl to rinse them.

'Can I wash the dolls' clothes too?' she asked.

Mother nodded. 'If you like,' she said.

'You will have to dry your hands before you undress your dolls, though.'

Sarah's hands and arms were still covered with soap suds, so she wiped them off on the towel. Her fingers felt funny and pinched; there were little hollows in them.

'Look, Mummy, my fingers have dimples in them!' cried Sarah.

Mother laughed. 'You've got washer-woman's hands, Sarah,' she said, 'and so have I. Just look at mine.' And Mother dried her hands and showed Sarah the funny pinched dimples on her fingertips. 'When we've finished all our washing we'll rub some hand lotion into our fingers.'

Sarah went and undressed Annie and Minnie, and washed their dresses, and their vests, and their pants and their socks. Oh, she was so busy. She had never been so busy.

Outside in her pram baby Carol began

to cry, so Mother dried her hands again and went to see what was the matter.

Sarah finished the clothes, and then she looked round for something else to wash. She dried her hands and went to look in the dolls' pram in case there was anything else to wash in there. Becky, the rag doll, did look dirty. Her dress was crumpled and grimy from when she had fallen out of the pram on a wet day and her face was smudged when Sarah had picked her up with muddy hands.

'Poor Becky,' said Sarah, taking her into the kitchen. 'I will wash you in the clothes tub and make you all new again,' and she plunged Becky into the lovely soapy suds.

Just then Mother came back. 'Look, Mummy,' said Sarah, 'I'm washing Becky!'

'Oh *Sarah*!' cried Mother. 'Don't you remember? She can't be bathed!'

'But I'm not bathing her,' said Sarah, 'I'm washing her, like the blankets.'

'I'm sure she'll be spoilt,' sighed Mother shaking her head, and she pulled Becky out of the soap suds. True enough, the colour in her dress and her face was blotched and streaked, and her filling was all lumpy, and in some places there was no filling left at all.

'Oh dear,' said Mother, and she squeezed Becky and thumped her. 'Perhaps she'll look better when she's dry.'

Mother laid Becky in the sunshine out-side the door, with a towel underneath her. 'We'll have to wait and see,' said Mother. 'Now let's hang out the washing.'

Sarah held the peg-bag for Mother while she hung the big blankets on the clothes-line and then Mother made a special little clothes-line for Sarah from the clothes post to the drainpipe. Sarah hung up all her blankets and Annie's and Minnie's clothes. Then Mother and Sarah both rubbed their washerwoman's hands with lotion, and it was time for dinner.

The washing danced on the two clothes-lines, and every time Mother went out to shake her blankets, she shook Becky and kneaded her stuffing. Becky began to look a bit better, but she was still wet at tea time when all the other washing was dry and Mother had ironed Annie's and Minnie's dresses.

When it was Sarah's bedtime, Becky was still wet. 'Will she be dry enough to take to bed?' she asked.

'No,' said Mother, 'I'm sure she won't.'

Sarah began to cry. 'She can't stay outside all night,' she sobbed. 'Can I put her in the pram?'

'Oh she's much too wet, Annie and Minnie wouldn't like that,' said Mother. 'I know, let's put her to bed in the airing cupboard, right next to the hot tank.'

So Becky was made comfortable on an old towel next to the tank, and Sarah took Annie to bed with her.

In the morning, Becky was dry and stiff. Mother rubbed her between her hands, and she became softer. Her filling was almost like before, but now she was too floppy, and her face and her clothes still looked worse than they had before she was washed. Sarah didn't like Becky any more.

'I know what we'll do,' said Mother. 'We'll write a letter to Grannie and tell her about Becky's bath. Perhaps she'll know what to do.'

So that morning, after baby Carol was in her pram, Mother wrote a letter to

Grannie telling her what had happened, and Sarah wrote a big kiss at the end of the letter. When they went shopping, Mother bought a stamp at the Post Office and Sarah stuck it on to the envelope before reaching up on tiptoe to push the letter into the letter-box.

There wasn't a letter from Grannie the next day, or the next, or the day after that, and Sarah began to get used to Becky being droopy and stained. She even took her to bed with her again. But the next day, what do you think? The Postman brought a parcel for Sarah, and inside the parcel were a new dress and some trousers for Becky and a letter for Sarah.

Mother read the letter. It said:

Dear Sarah,

Here is a new dress for Becky and some trousers to cover her legs. Mummy can snip the stitches of the spoilt dress and take it off, and you can put this one on instead. When I come to stay, I'll make Becky a new inside, and a new face if she needs one.

With fondest love from Grannie.

Wasn't Sarah a lucky girl? Mother soon had Becky's old clothes off and Sarah dressed her in her new ones, and she was nearly as good as new, but not quite. And next time Sarah had a washing day she didn't put Becky in the wash tub.

'Poor Becky,' she said 'You can't have a bath like a baby, and you can't have a wash like the clothes.' But she still liked her best, and took her to bed with her every night.

4. Jeannie and Jojo

Jeannie had a very special doll called Jojo. Jeannie loved Jojo. She had real hair which Jeannie could comb, and eyes that opened and shut, and she had two dresses, a blue woolly one Mother had knitted and a red one made from the same material as one of Jeannie's dresses. But that wasn't why she was a special doll. Jojo was very special because she had belonged to Mother when she was a little girl.

When Jeannie was nearly four she used to play with Susan. Susan had a doll with shutting eyes and real hair and of course Jeannie longed for a doll like that too. She talked and talked about that doll.

And then one day it was Jeannie's birthday, and Mother and Father had given her a wooden cradle, just like a real baby's, with blankets and a mattress, a pillow and an eiderdown in it.

Jeannie liked the cot, and she put her teddy in it, and played being a nurse all the morning.

Just before dinner, the doorbell rang, 'Ding dong!' Mother opened the door and there was Grandma.

'How's my birthday girl?' asked Grandma, and after she'd hugged Jeannie and taken off her coat, she sat down in the kitchen with her big zip bag.

'I've got a surprise for you in here,' said Grandma.

Jeannie began jumping up and down. 'Ooh!' she said, clasping her hands together. 'What is it?'

'What is it I hear that you want most of all then?' said Grandma. Jeannie just looked at Grandma. 'Is it a doll with hair

and eyes that open and shut?' asked Grandma.

'Ooh!' said Jeannie, more excited than
ever.

Grandma put her hand inside the bag.
There was a box inside.

'Pull it out then,' said Grandma. Jeannie
brought out the box. It had string round it.

'Let me have it here,' said Grandma, and
she put the box on the table and lifted
Jeannie on to her lap.

Grandma said, 'When Mummy was a
little girl a bit bigger than you, she had a
doll with real hair and eyes that opened
and shut. She called her Jojo. She loved
Jojo and took her everywhere with her.
Then she grew to be a big girl, too big for
dolls, and she put Jojo away in a drawer,
wrapped up in a shawl, and she stayed
there for a long long while.

'Then I heard you were longing for a

doll with eyes that open and shut and real hair, and I remembered Jojo. The only thing is . . .' and Grandma looked at Jeannie, 'she isn't like your other dolls. When Mummy was a little girl dolls weren't made of plastic, and if you drop Jojo on anything hard, she'll break. I wonder if you are big enough to have a doll like that. Are you?' Jeannie nodded; her eyes grew big.

'Is she in the box?'

'You undo it and see,' said Grandma and she helped Jeannie to undo the string.

In a minute the lid of the box was off, and there, on a bed of white tissue paper, was Jojo, in a red dress that matched the one Grandma had made Jeannie for Christmas.

'Oh!' breathed Jeannie and hugged her tightly.

'Now, you must remember to be careful with her,' said Grandma.

'Oh yes!' said Jeannie and she took Jojo very carefully and put her to bed in the new cradle.

So Jeannie loved Jojo as much as Mother had done. She took her everywhere and she took great care of her. She even put her on a chair beside her at meal-times, and laid a doll's cup, saucer and plate for her. Yes, Jojo was a very special doll. And whenever Jeannie went to the park or to the shops, Jojo went too, in the dolls' pram, and of course Jeannie took her to Susan's – you remember Susan had a doll with hair and shutting eyes, too.

But one day, a dreadful thing happened. Susan's brother Barry had a car, a big one for sitting in, with pedals that made it go along quite fast. He had it for his birthday and Jeannie did want a ride. Now Barry and Susan had a garden swing and while Jeannie waited for Barry to let her have a go, she sat inside the safety bars of the swing holding Jojo and watching Barry race up and down.

At last, Barry got tired of that and said Jeannie could have a turn while he fixed up a piece of rope on the clothes post for a petrol pump. Jeannie climbed out of the swing very carefully and sat Jojo against the side and wrapped her shawl round her. Then she jumped into the car and drove it round and round just like Barry.

But, oh dear! Suddenly there was a thump and a cracking sound, and Jeannie was just in time to see the swing move gently in the breeze – without Jojo in it!

Jojo had slipped and then slid through the bars and on to the concrete under the swing. Her head was broken and there was a hole in one side of her cheek.

How Jeannie cried. Susan's mother heard her and came outside to see what was

the matter. 'Oh my!' she said. 'Oh dear, oh dear!' and then when Jeannie didn't stop crying, 'Let's go and find your Mummy.'

She took Jeannie and Jojo home and Mother said, 'Oh my!' and 'Oh dear, oh dear!' and then she said, 'I wonder.'

'Look,' said Jeannie's mother, 'there's just a chance someone could mend Jojo.'

Mother washed Jeannie's face and dried her eyes and put on Jeannie's coat and her own coat and wrapped Jojo's shawl round her to hide her poor broken head. They went on the bus to town and Jeannie just sat and held Jojo while Mother put her arm round her.

Jeannie had stopped crying, but she still sobbed a little and her throat hurt. When they reached town, Mother and Jeannie got off the bus and Mother led the way down a side street Jeannie had never seen. Soon they came to a little shop with a window just full of dolls and teddy bears. There were dolls of all sizes, big baby dolls, costume dolls, teenage dolls, black dolls, pink dolls, dolls with hair and dolls without. And on a shelf above the dolls was a row of dolls' heads, yes, just heads.

'This is a dolls' hospital,' said Mother, 'and I hope the mending man will be able to find a new head for Jojo.'

Jeannie didn't say anything; she followed Mother into the shop. Inside there seemed to be hundreds more dolls and teddies and heads, and arms and legs too, and wigs of hair, and pairs of eyes . . . A little old man came out of the door behind the counter.

'Hello my dear,' he said, 'has your dolly had an accident?' Jeannie nodded, and Mother pushed back the shawl.

'Let the gentleman see,' she said. Jeannie held up Jojo and showed the gentleman her poor head.

'She was mine when I was a girl,' said Mother. 'I wonder if you would be able to fit a new head on a doll like this?'

'Let me have her a minute,' said the little old man, and he put his finger inside Jojo's broken head and fiddled with the hooks and bands inside until he could take the head off altogether.

'Now let me see,' he muttered. 'I think . . .' and he went away to look in a drawer. He came back with a doll's head with shutting eyes – but no hair.

Jeannie began to cry again. 'She hasn't any hair,' she sobbed. But Mr Simpson was talking to Mother. He was used to little girls with broken dolls.

'Yes, Madam, I'm sure I can fix her up. You will hardly know the difference. Her hair will be nylon of course, and that'll be better for the little girl to wash and comb – and today's paints make a more delicate colouring possible. Oh yes, you leave her with me, I can promise her for tomorrow at lunchtime.'

'There now!' said Mother, 'isn't Mr Simpson a clever man! Jojo will be even better than before.'

So Jeannie had to leave Jojo in the shop – and Mother and Jeannie had to hurry home and cook the tea and light the fire before Daddy came home.

'Well,' said Daddy, 'what have you been doing today?' He did have a surprise when he heard about the dolls' hospital.

That night Jeannie had to go to bed without tucking up Jojo and next morning she kept asking how soon they could go into town. At last it was time, and Mother and Jeannie went down the road to catch the bus. When they reached the dolls' hospital, and Mother opened the door, Jeannie rushed inside. There on the counter was Jojo. Her dark hair looked even better than before, and her face looked even more real. Otherwise, she was just the same and Jeannie hugged her tightly, while Mother paid Mr Simpson.

So Jojo got her new head and was as good as ever. And do you know, when Grandma came next time she didn't notice anything at all – and then when Jeannie told her, she said, 'I remember taking Mummy to that same shop to get Jojo mended when she was a little girl. But that time, we had to have different hair. Mr Simpson hadn't any fair hair, and Jojo had to become a dark doll. So you're luckier than Mummy was!'

And Jeannie laughed and said, 'Yes, and I think Jojo's happy too.'

5. Michael's Chicken-pox Game

Michael was miserable. He had chicken-pox. His back itched and his tummy itched and his legs itched, and Mummy said he mustn't scratch the spots.

He sat up in bed and played with his bricks on a tray and sometimes he set out his train on the floor, but he had to stay in the bedroom so that his baby sister Jane wouldn't catch the chicken-pox.

Big brother Jonathan had had chicken-pox long ago when Michael was a baby, so when he wasn't at school they played together in the bedroom. And when Jane was asleep, Mummy came and read stories and played with Michael. But when Mummy was busy and Jonathan was at school,

Michael was very miserable indeed . . . except when Mrs Black came to see him.

Mrs Black lived next door to Michael and Jonathan. She was older than their mother, but not as old as Grandma and her children were grown up now and worked. When she heard Michael had chicken-pox, she knew his mother wouldn't be able to do her shopping or take Jane for a ride in her pram because then Michael would have to be left alone in bed. So every morning at 11 o'clock, Mrs Black came over to see Michael, and Michael's mother and the baby went down to the shops.

Now one day Michael was specially miserable; his spots were specially itchy and he really didn't want to play with his bricks or his jigsaws or his cars. He looked at his books and he wished Mummy would come and read to him. He pushed his fire-engine up and down the bed cover:

'Urr-urr, urr-urr,' he made the siren noise. But he was hot and the sun was shining and he did so wish he was outside or with his friends at Playgroup.

Then he heard a knock at the back door and the sound of it opening. 'Coo-ee!' called Mrs Black.

Michael heard Mummy call back, 'Can you go on up, Mrs Black? I'm nearly ready.' And then she called more loudly up the stairs, 'Good-bye, Michael. I won't be long. Mrs Black's here!'

Mrs Black came upstairs and the corner stair on the landing creaked. Then tap, tap, 'Can I come in, Michael?' called Mrs Black. 'Here I am. How are all those spots, then?'

Michael opened his pyjama jacket and showed Mrs Black the spots on his chest. 'Poor old chap,' said Mrs Black, 'but you'll soon be better. In a few days' time they'll all go away and you'll be able to go to Playgroup again. I wonder what your friends are doing there now? What do you like doing best?'

Michael thought hard. Did he like painting best? Or the clay? Or the lovely yellow sand?

'I know!' he said. 'It's the water I like best. There are pots and bottles and tubes and things . . .'

'I expect you'd like to play with water now while you're feeling so itchy,' nodded Mrs Black. 'Just thinking about water makes you feel cooler you know.' So Mrs Black began to talk about the seaside and the things her children who were big boys now used to do when they went on their holidays.

Quite soon Mummy came back from the shops and it was time for Mrs Black to go home and cook her dinner.

'I've a good idea for something you can do,' said Mummy after Mrs Black had gone. 'When I was down at the shops I met Andrew's Mummy,' (Andrew was one of Michael's Playgroup friends) 'and she told me that when Andrew and his brother had chicken-pox they used to have lovely times in the bath. She put some special powder in the water to soothe the chicken-pox spots and they used to play in it for ages. Would you like to play in the bath?'

Michael thought that was a marvellous idea so Mummy went to run some water into the bath – not too hot, not too cold, but just right for Michael to sit in. It was warm in the bathroom; the sun shone through the window. Mummy poured a cup full of soothing powder into the water and Michael put in his boats, his plastic ball and a beaker.

It was fun in the bath; Michael lay on

his tummy and poured water into his boat
till it sank, and he blew the ball along the
top of the water, and forgot all about his
spots. He lay on his back and blew the ball
down to his toes. Then he poured water on

his tummy and behind the boat so that it moved along in the water.

Mummy was back saying it was time for him to come out to be dried and have his spots powdered long before Michael was tired of the bath, and he felt quite hungry when he saw his dinner.

Mrs Black came to see Michael the next day as well, and you can guess what he talked to her about, can't you? But what do you think Mrs Black said? She said:

'I've brought a surprise for you today,' and she gave Michael a parcel tied up with string.

The string was tied in a bow. Michael pulled the ends to undo it. Then he pulled off the paper and inside there was a box. Michael lifted the lid and there inside was – what do you think? – a coil of plastic tubing, a little red jug, an aluminium teapot, an empty plastic squash bottle and a funnel!

'Ooh!' cried Michael. 'These are just like we have at Playgroup in the water tray. I can have them in the bath. Oh, Mrs Black, Mummy will be surprised – how did you know about them?'

'Aha,' said Mrs Black. 'When I saw your mother in the garden yesterday after dinner she told me about how you'd enjoyed your bath and then when I went to the shops I met your Playgroup lady and she asked how you were. So I told her about playing in the bath and she told me about the wonderful time you have at Playgroup with all the exciting things in the water tray. So I thought I would get some of those things for you to enjoy in your bath at home.'

When Mummy came back, Michael had a wonderful game in the bath. He put his funnel into one end of the tube and the tube into the plastic squash bottle and he poured water into it from the teapot; then he ran water straight into the funnel from the teapot. Sometimes he blew bubbles through the tubes and sometimes he filled the teapot and poured water all over himself. He quite forgot about his chicken-pox.

When Mummy came to dry him they put all the new water toys in her nylon shopping bag and hung it over the bath to drip dry.

Next day Michael was much better, but he still had a good long play in the bath with all his new water toys and even when he was quite better he still liked to use them in the bath, though of course he could play with them in the sink then, and in the garden too.

Somebody else liked that collection of water play toys. Can you guess who that was? Yes, big brother Jonathan thought the tube and the funnel and the big bottle and the teapot made bathtimes much more interesting, and sometimes Jonathan and Michael played with them together.

So Michael's chicken-pox wasn't all bad, was it?

Note: The soothing powder used in the bath was bicarbonate of soda: two cupfuls to be added to a small bath, one to a baby bath. A young child should obviously not be left alone in a bath for long, an adult should be in earshot.

6. Jeannie's Holiday at Home

Jeannie sat on the kitchen step with her big doll Jojo on her lap. Mother was busy washing and the cat had just jumped over the wall to visit the next door's cat. Jeannie did wish Susan was here. Susan lived across the road, and most mornings Jeannie played with her. But Susan, her brother Barry, and their Mummy and Daddy had gone away to the seaside for a holiday.

'When will Susan be back?' Jeannie asked.

Mother laughed. 'She only went yesterday,' she said. 'And they've gone for a fortnight, that's two whole weeks . . . Why don't you play at taking Jojo and Teddy to the sea?'

Jeannie thought that was a good idea. She found her little case and packed it with

Jojo's other dress and a bow for Teddy.
Then she went to the toy cupboard and
took out the dolls' cups, saucers and plates
and put them in her basket.

'Where's your seaside to be?' asked
Mother.

'Down the garden by my sandpit,' said
Jeannie, and she carried her case and
basket through the kitchen and put them
on the path beside the back door. Then she
went into the shed and brought out two
huge cardboard cartons.

'This is the car,' she explained and she
put the cartons side by side on the path.

Jeannie came back indoors, took Teddy
and Jojo out of the dolls' pram with some
of their blankets and sat them in one of the
boxes. The she clambered into the other
one with her case and basket.

'Bye-bye, Mummy,' she called. 'Brrum,
brrum, brrum,' and the 'car' was off.

'Here we are,' she shouted presently, and
scrambling out of the 'car' she picked up
Jojo and Teddy, the blanket, the case and
the basket and made her way to the other
end of the garden where the sandpit was.

A row of runner-beans grew next to the

sandpit and hid her from the house. Jeannie sat Jojo and Teddy so they leant against the runner-bean sticks, unpacked her basket and began to set out a picnic for them. Then she took off her shoes and socks and sat wriggling her toes in the sand, trying to remember what the seaside was like.

The sand was warm and soft. She began to play with it, running it through her fingers and lifting her hands so that she could see it fall in a golden shower on to her legs.

'Hello, Mrs Perkins!' It was Mother's voice. 'Fancy meeting you here. I have come to pick some runner-beans for dinner, though I never saw any beans growing on a beach before. Are you coming up to the Beach Café for a cup of milk and a biscuit?'

Jeannie followed her back up the path and suddenly she saw what Mother meant.

Out in the garden were a small table and two chairs. There was a red cloth on the table, two glasses and a plate of biscuits.

'This is our Beach Café!' said Mother. She and Jeannie both had a glass of milk and then Jeannie helped Mother slice the beans.

'I know what we'll do,' said Mother. 'We'll pretend we're on holiday! We'll have our dinner in the garden. I don't think we can sit on your beach, we'll eat here on our own seaside balcony. When you've collected Jojo and Teddy from the beach you can lay the table for me.'

Mother went indoors to cook the runner-beans and Jeannie ran down the garden to Jojo and Teddy.

'Time to pack up,' she said. 'It's nearly dinner-time at our holiday house.' She picked up the cups and saucers together with Jojo and Teddy and the blanket.

'You can have a holiday dinner too,' she said, as she carried them up the garden and sat them carefully on the grass near to the 'seaside balcony' dinner table. She went indoors.

'What can I have for a table for Jojo and Teddy?' she asked.

'I should use a box out of the shed,' said Mother. So Jeannie went to find the box, and then she went back into the shed and found the groundsheet and put the box in the middle of the groundsheet.

'May I have a table-cloth?' she called.

'I think a tea-cloth would be a better size,' said Mother, coming to the door, and she went inside and brought back a new blue one from the cupboard. Jeannie spread it over the box. She fetched her own stool from the dining-room and two of the dolls' pillows for cushions for Teddy. Then she laid her little table with the

plates and other things out of her basket.
After that she went indoors for the big
knives and forks and laid the seaside balcony table for Mother and herself.

Mother served the dinner and together
they carried their plates out into the garden and sat at the table.

'This is very enjoyable,' said Mother.
'Nearly as good as the real seaside, and the
holiday house serves the kind of food we
like, too.'

Jeannie laughed. It was fun eating dinner in the garden. When they had finished,
Mother brought out ice-cream and glasses
of fruit juice on a tray and it really did feel
like a holiday.

'It's much too warm to be indoors,' said
Mother. 'We'll go on having our holiday.
As soon as I've washed up we'll make a
picnic. We'll go to the paddling pool in the
park and pretend that is the seaside. You

can take your swimsuit and your boat and I'll take my knitting and a book and we'll sit in the sun and get brown. You don't need to go to the real seaside to have a holiday.'

Jeannie jumped up and down with excitement. She fetched Jojo and Teddy in from the garden and put them in the pram for a sleep and then she helped make the sandwiches for the picnic. Mother put the sandwiches in her basket and Jeannie put biscuits into her little one. Mother helped Jeannie find her swimsuit and a towel and Jeannie found her boat. Soon they were walking along the road and down two more roads to the park.

They walked past the flower beds and the people playing tennis, past the men playing bowls and the big boys playing cricket and came to the corner of the park where the paddling pool was. There were other mothers and children there: some of them were in swimsuits and they were running in and out of the water shouting and splashing. There were others on the edge of the water or playing games under the trees. Some of the mothers were sitting talking and some had babies on their laps.

It was a happy place. Just like the seaside, Jeannie thought.

Jeannie pulled off her shoes and socks and Mother helped her with her swimsuit. She ran down to the water and tried it with her foot. It was warm. Soon she was running across the pool splashing as she went. Some other children followed her and they all ran round and round the pool and across it and up and down the grassy banks, till they were tired out. Puffing and laughing, they ran back to their mothers, but after a little rest one of them came over to Jeannie where she was sitting beside Mother.

'What's your name?' asked the little girl.

'Jeannie,' said Jeannie. 'What's yours?'

'I'm Sarah,' replied the little girl. 'Will

you come and look for fir cones?' There were some big fir trees the other side of the paddling pool and Mother could see them from where she sat.

'Let's take the biscuits out of your basket,' said Mother, 'then you can use it for fir cones.' Sarah had a bucket for hers.

Sarah and Jeannie ran off to the trees. There were lots of fir cones there and they were soon very busy filling their bucket and basket. When they ran back to the edge of the pool they found their mothers had started talking together. Sarah's Mother had a baby in a pram. Jeannie and Sarah put their fir cones down and ran off to the pool again.

When they came back, Jeannie's mother was knitting and Sarah's mother was making a daisy-chain for the baby. Sarah and Jeannie played tea parties with the fir cones and then they all ate their picnic together. Mother didn't read her book at all, but she did tell Jeannie and Sarah a story while Sarah's mother saw to the baby. Then it was time to go home.

'It was a lovely day,' Jeannie told Daddy that night and Mother said, 'We are having a little holiday at home while the sun shines.'

So they did. Every weekday Jeannie played seasides in the garden with Jojo and Teddy and had her milk at the Beach Café and her dinner at the seaside balcony and then helped Mother make a picnic tea to take to the park. Mother would sit by the pool with Sarah's mother while Jeannie and Sarah paddled and raced with the other children. Sometimes Jeannie brought Jojo and Sarah brought her big doll and they played picnics with the fir cones.

When Susan and Barry came home from their holiday, they had a lot to say about the seaside and their holiday house and then Jeannie told them about the park and the pool and her new friend Sarah and that very afternoon they all went to the park together.

'It's just as good as being at the seaside,' said Susan.

And Jeannie said, 'We had a lovely holiday at home.'

NOTE

In these two stories about Mother going into hospital, note especially that Peter's father stays at home when Mother goes to hospital to have the baby, and that the children visit her and the baby in hospital. When Jeannie's mother has an operation, Jeannie doesn't visit her, grandmother comes to stay, and father visits mother every night taking gifts and messages. If mother is likely to go to hospital, it is important that the reader should find out what will be possible about visiting and alter the story to suit.

7 Peter Paints a Secret

When Peter's mother went to hospital to have a new baby, Daddy stayed at home with Peter and his big sister Ann. Ann went to school every day, so Peter and Daddy had to look after everything themselves.

On the first morning, after Ann had gone to school and Peter and Daddy had made the beds and washed the dishes, Daddy said, 'What do you think I ought to do now?'

And Peter said, 'What are we going to have for dinner?'

'We'll have to go to the shops and buy something,' said Daddy. So Peter found the shopping basket and Daddy locked the door and they went to the shops.

Daddy bought some bread and some

cheese at the grocer's and some apples and bananas at the fruit shop. The next shop sold paint and wallpaper. Daddy stopped to look in the window.

'I know!' he said, 'let's give Mummy a big surprise. Let's decorate the bedroom while she's away.'

They went inside. On the counter were big books full of pieces of wallpaper. There was shiny paper, paper with stripes and swirls and spots. There was even some that looked like wood. Peter soon found one he liked, but Daddy didn't think Mummy would want cowboys in her bedroom, so he chose some paper with flowers on it instead. He bought five rolls of wallpaper, a tin of blue paint and a bag of paste. Peter carried the paste all the way home.

As soon as they had put the shopping away, Daddy got down to work. He took the curtains off their hooks and folded them up. He rolled up the mats and put them under the bed. Then he put everything else on top of the bed and covered it over with an old sheet.

'That's that,' said Daddy. 'Now to wash off the old paper.'

He filled a bucket with water and found a cloth and big flat tool for scraping.

'Can I help?' asked Peter.

Daddy looked at him. 'No, it's too messy,' he said. 'You play with your things and I'll soon have it done.'

Peter went and fetched his bricks from the cupboard downstairs. Suddenly, he wished Mummy was at home. They hadn't had a drink or a story, and it didn't seem as if there was going to be any dinner either! He carried the box of bricks upstairs and began to make brick trains on the window-sill.

Daddy was having a lovely time, slop-

ping water on to the wall and scratching it
with his scraper tool so that the old wallpaper came off in wet wiggly bits. Peter
watched. He wished he could have a go.

'Let me help,' he asked again.

'Not with this,' said Daddy.

Peter sighed deeply. 'When will it be
dinner-time?' he asked.

'Oh bother my boots!' cried Daddy. 'I
quite forgot about dinner. Tell you what,'
he said, seeing Peter's face, 'I won't stop to
cook any dinner. We'll go and buy some
fish and chips when we're hungry. But
now I want to get on with this. What would
you like to do while I'm busy?'

'Paint,' said Peter, as that was the first
thing he thought of.

'Where is your paint, then?' asked Daddy.

'Mummy makes it,' said Peter. Daddy
put down his scraper, wiped his hands and
looked at Peter. 'How?' he asked.

'I don't know,' said Peter, 'with flour and water and little bottles of coloured stuff...'

'Tell you what,' said Daddy, 'go and find your boots and Mummy's washing apron, and you'd better be my mate after all!'

The rest of the morning was lovely. First Peter slopped water on to the wall with a sponge while Daddy scraped and then he had a short turn with the scraper himself. They nearly forgot all about dinner and it was only when they went to fetch a fresh bucket of water that Daddy looked at the clock.

'Bother my boots!' said Daddy, 'we'd better hurry.' He helped Peter pull off his wellingtons and found another shirt for him because he'd got very wet even with Mummy's apron round him. Then they hurried down to the shops.

'You're just in time,' laughed the Fish-and-Chip Man. He scooped the golden chips into two bags and put two crunchy pieces of fish on a sheet of paper. 'You've got the last lot. Salt and vinegar?'

Daddy nodded and the Fish-and-Chip Man shook salt and vinegar into the bags and on to the fish before wrapping them all up in newspaper. Peter wanted to carry the newspaper parcel home. It was warm to touch, and it smelt delicious. But he hadn't gone far before it felt too hot to hold, and he handed it over to Daddy.

After they had eaten their fish and chips, Daddy said, 'Now I'm going to rub down the doors and round the windows with sandpaper, to make it smooth for painting, but I don't think you should do this bit because you'll get very dusty.'

Daddy tied one of his big handkerchiefs over his hair and Peter played garages with his bricks and a toy car, but it wasn't very interesting. Then he went under the bed where the mats were, and pretended to be camping, but that didn't last long either. The room seemed full of dust and Daddy was covered in whitish specks.

Peter went over to watch. 'You have a go at the skirting board, then,' said Daddy after he had fallen over Peter three times, and he gave Peter a piece of the yellow paper with a scratchy side. Peter rubbed and rubbed. He didn't know whether to go round and round or up and down, but Daddy said it didn't matter, any way would make the wood ready for painting.

At last Daddy said, 'Well, that'll do. Let's clean up and go to meet Ann.'

So they met Ann and had tea and then the telephone rang. When Daddy came back he was all smiles. 'That was Mummy,' he said. 'You've got a new little brother.

Tomorrow we can all go and see her and the baby after school, and Mummy's told me how to make your paint.'

Next day, Peter helped Daddy quickly with the housework and then they washed off the rest of the wallpaper and wiped down all the wood they had rubbed so hard with the sandpaper.

'Now,' said Daddy, 'I'm going to stir the paint I bought for the doors and windows.' He found a piece of wood and opened the tin, and then he stirred and stirred with the piece of wood till all the lumps had gone. It was like stirring a blue pudding, Peter thought.

'Which bit can I paint?' he asked.

'Ah-ha!' teased Daddy, 'you can paint the wall.'

'But I thought the wallpaper was for the wall,' said Peter.

'All in good time,' said Daddy mysteriously. 'Well, I think that's mixed. And here's my brush. And here's a brush for you.' He gave Peter a real painter's brush, just like the one he was going to use for the doors and windows.

'And here', said Daddy, reaching up to the saucepan shelf, 'is the paint for you.' And he brought down Ann's and Peter's seaside buckets. One had red paint inside and the other one had green.

'Let's take it upstairs,' said Daddy. 'Carefully now, mind the carpet. Now,' he said, when the two buckets of Peter's paint and the tin of Daddy's paint were safely in the bedroom, 'yesterday you wanted to paint and I didn't know how to make your paint, but Mummy told me last night. The paint in the buckets is your kind of paint and it won't spoil your clothes.'

'I'll need some paper,' said Peter.

'Now what did I say downstairs?' asked

Daddy, 'didn't I say you could paint the walls? You helped me clean off all that old paper and I won't want to put the new paper on till I've painted all the woodwork. There are four lovely white walls for you to paint on, better than any paper. Come on, let's see what you can do.'

So, while Daddy put his blue paint on the door, Peter made patterns and shapes and lines as high as he could reach on the wall round the windows. Some were red, some were green and some mixed up together. There was so much wall to cover, he had to stand on tiptoe and make great sweeps above his head.

He and Daddy both had a very busy day; they only stopped for fish and chips, and worked all the afternoon until it was time to meet Ann and go to see Mummy.

'Now remember,' said Daddy, as they went up to the hospital to see Mummy and

the new baby, 'you mustn't tell Mummy about doing the bedroom, that's a secret.'

Later on, after they had said 'hello' to the baby, and Peter and Ann were both cuddled up close to Mummy on her bed in the hospital, Mummy asked Peter, 'What. have you and Daddy been doing all day?'

'We've been doing jobs,' began Peter importantly. He looked at Daddy, and Daddy winked at him. 'I've been painting,' he said. But he didn't say what kind of painting.

The next day Daddy painted and painted round the windows and Peter painted and painted on the next wall, and the day after that Daddy began to stick the wallpaper on the walls Peter had painted. Soon there was only one strip left to paper, and at last all Peter's painting was covered up.

Peter nearly felt sad that his painting had disappeared, but as Daddy said, it was really a special kind of secret. Underneath the little blue and white flowers were wonderful swirly patterns and only the two of them knew they were there.

'Mummy's coming home tomorrow,' said Daddy 'and we'll show her our surprise.'

And when Mummy saw the room, my goodness she *was* surprised. In fact she thought they had made such a good job of it that they ought to do the sitting-room next. 'And then, Peter,' she said, 'your new brother and I can share the secret too.'

8 Jeannie and Grandma Keep House

When Jeannie's mother had to go to hospital, Grandma came to look after Jeannie and her father.

'You must show Grandma where we keep everything, like the cups and plates, and the brushes and the bread,' Mother had said, and she wrote out a note for Grandma which she left in the kitchen about which shops to go to and which days the baker called and when the milkman had to be paid.

On Grandma's first day alone with Jeannie, Grandma had to keep asking questions like, 'Where are the basins, Jeannie? Where does Mummy keep the flour?' and 'Do you know where the carpet sweeper is?' and Jeannie ran and found all of them. They did laugh when Grandma looked for the whisk and cooking apron in the drawer where the tea-towels were kept.

That afternoon Grandma let Jeannie make a little cake of her own when she was making a big cake for tea, and she made enough pastry for Jeannie to make six jam tarts as well. When Daddy went to hospital to see Mummy that night, Grandma said, 'Tell Mummy Jeannie and I have been busy cooking.'

Next day, Grandma said they should go to the shops and Jeannie would have to show her which was their Butcher and which was their Grocer.

Jeannie danced along with her little basket on her arm, saying 'This way, Grandma.' When they reached the crossing place she showed Grandma how to use

the button to make the traffic lights turn red to stop the cars.

'See Grandma,' she said, 'the red man is shining now. We must wait till he goes in and the green man comes out and then we can cross the road.'

After a few minutes the red man went in and the green man came out; the cars stopped and Jeannie and Grandma crossed the road. (This kind of crossing is called a pelican crossing. Have you got a pelican crossing where you go shopping?)

They walked past the shops until they came to one with meat in the window. 'This is the shop we go to,' said Jeannie.

'Robertson's, Butcher,' read Grandma from the sign over the window. 'Yes,' she said. 'That was the name on Mummy's list.'

Jeannie skipped through the open doorway. 'Hello, Mr Robertson,' she called. 'This is my Grandma.'

'Good morning, Madam,' said Mr Robertson. 'How's your daughter-in-law?' Mr Robertson meant Jeannie's Mummy, and Grandma said she was getting on very well, thank you.

When they had finished in the Butcher's, they went to the Grocer's and then Grandma said: 'Let's go to that fruit shop with the flowers in the window.'

'Oh!' said Jeannie. 'Mummy doesn't go in there, she says it costs too much.'

'I expect she's right,' said Grandma. 'But I don't think the other greengrocer sells flowers and I thought we'd buy a bunch of flowers for Daddy to take to her tonight; that would be nice, wouldn't it?'

'Oh yes,' smiled Jeannie, so Grandma led the way and Jeannie followed.

'How much are the freesias?' asked Grandma. The young lady assistant told her and Grandma said she would buy two bunches; the assistant took the lovely mauve and yellow and white flowers out of the metal vase in the window and carefully wrapped them up in tissue paper so the stems were covered and a kind of hood of paper was left behind the flowers to keep out the cold. She carefully folded this over and pinned it so the flowers were all inside their warm white paper.

'How about a little bunch of flowers for you to send, Jeannie?' asked Grandma. 'I see they have lily-of-the-valley and violets – which would you like to buy?'

Jeannie looked at the bunches of white flowers like rows of tiny bells with thin dark green stalks which Grandma said were the lily-of-the-valley, and at the rich blue, velvety flowers with the heart-shaped leaves which Grandma called violets. They were both so pretty.

'Smell them, dear,' suggested Grandma,

and Jeannie put her nose close to the violets and took a long sniff. She thought for a moment of woods and hedges. It was a sweet, gentle smell. Mummy would like it. Then she smelt the lilies, and stopped, puzzled. Where had she smelt that smell before? It was like a cool damp garden, but ... she had smelt that smell indoors. In the bathroom, that was it, when Mummy had had a bath ... 'They smell like Mummy's powder,' she said. 'She'll like these.'

'We'll take a bunch of the lily-of-the-valley,' said Grandma, so the shop assistant wrapped them up just like Grandma's freesias and Jeannie laid her little bunch gently in her basket.

As soon as they were home, Jeannie and Grandma put their flowers in water. Jeannie found a tall thin vase for Grandma's freesias and a short thin one for her lilies-of-the-valley. After dinner, Grandma wrote a card to go with her flowers, then she gave a card to Jeannie, who coloured it blue and wrote an 'x' for a kiss and a 'J' for Jeannie on it. Daddy took the flowers with him when he went to see Mummy and he brought back a kiss for Jeannie.

*

Next day, Grandma looked at the list Mummy had left in her kitchen and said, 'I see it's the day we pay the milkman. I don't know what time he comes so I'll put the money out now while I remember.' She put two 50p pieces on the top of the cupboard near the back door.

'Miaou!' It was Monty the cat. 'Miaou!'

'Monty wants some milk,' said Jeannie.

'So he does,' said Grandma. 'You give him some.'

Jeannie fetched Monty's clean saucer and

a jug of milk and poured out a saucerful
for Monty. Carefully, she put it down on
the floor in Monty's usual place by the
cupboard. She watched as he lapped it,

and the tip of his black tail quivered with
pleasure. Monty never drank all his milk
at once. When he had drunk enough, he
licked his whiskers and his paws and then
jumped up on the cupboard to look out of
the window. He began to wash himself and

that reminded Grandma that she was going to wash Jeannie's hair so they went upstairs to the bathroom.

They had just finished washing Jeannie's hair when there was a knock at the back door. 'That must be the milkman,' said Grandma, and she wrapped a towel round Jeannie's head before going down to answer the door. Jeannie followed.

Grandma opened the back door. 'Just a minute, Milkman,' she said. 'I have your money ready.'

But it wasn't on the cupboard where Grandma had put it. 'I did put it there, didn't I, Jeannie – two 50p pieces,' said Grandma. She couldn't believe her eyes. She and Jeannie looked on the table and on the windowsill and on the ledge over the boiler. But they couldn't find the two 50p pieces anywhere.

Grandma gave the milkman a pound

note from her purse, and when he had gone Jeannie and Grandma went on looking.

'Well I don't know,' said Grandma, 'I really don't. I'll sweep the floor. Perhaps I'll find it then.' So Jeannie found the broom for Grandma and the brush and dustpan, and Grandma carefully swept the floor. There were no coins under the table, or in a corner, or under the mats.

'Pick up Monty's saucer, Jeannie,' said Grandma. 'He won't want his milk all dusty, will he?'

Jeannie picked up the cat's saucer and put it on the table. She still had the towel round her head – you remember she had just had her hair washed.

'You can put it down now,' said Grandma. As Jeannie bent down to put the saucer on the floor, the towel came unwound, and the end went into the saucer of milk.

'Oh!' cried Jeannie. 'My towel's coming off and the end of it is in Monty's saucer!' She flicked it out and what do you think? The towel had soaked up most of the milk and there in the bottom of the saucer were the two 50p pieces!

'Look Grandma, Look!' she cried. 'Look in Monty's saucer!'

Grandma looked. And Grandma laughed. 'Monty hid them,' she said between her laughs. 'What a funny cat you've got!'

'How did Monty hide them?' Jeannie wanted to know.

'He must have knocked them off the cupboard when he jumped down from there while we were upstairs washing your hair,' explained Grandma, 'and they must have fallen right into his saucer.'

Just then Monty walked into the kitchen and went up to his milk saucer. 'Miaou,' he said, 'miaou – where's the milk I left?'

Jeannie stroked him and said, 'Did you knock Grandma's money off the cupboard, Monty? Did you know it was there, or did you hide it? Grandma says you are a funny cat!'

When Daddy came home, Jeannie and Grandma told him about Monty and the money, and Daddy laughed too and said he would tell Mummy.

'Mummy did enjoy hearing about Monty and the milk money,' said Daddy later. 'She's feeling much better and she'll be coming home on Sunday.'

When Mummy came home she had to rest and Grandma stayed for a few days to help her. Grandma and Jeannie told Mummy all the things they had done while she was away; they told her about the cooking, and about buying the flowers, and they told her about how Jeannie had shown Grandma the way the pelican crossing worked – but the thing they talked about most was Monty and the milk money.

The next time the milkman came, Grandma said: 'Do you remember I couldn't find your money when you came last week? Well . . .'

'You'll never guess where they found it,' laughed Mummy from the chair where she was sitting.

'Had the cat eaten it?' asked the milkman with a wink.

'Not quite,' said Grandma, but as she told the milkman about finding it in Monty's saucer, 'Well I never did!' laughed the milkman. 'Monty the Milk Money Mog, eh?' and he laughed again. Every time he came after that, he'd say, 'Have you got the money, or has the cat hidden it today?'

Monty just flicked his tail and blinked. He didn't care what the milkman called him so long as he brought his milk every day.

SEE YOU AT THE MATCH

Margaret Joy

Six delightful stories about football. Whether spectator, player, winner or loser, these short, easy stories for young readers are a must for all football fans.

RAGDOLLY ANNA'S CIRCUS

Jean Kenward

Made only from a morsel of this and a tatter of that, Ragdolly Anna is a very special doll. These adventures of the popular doll are based on the television series.

CHRIS AND THE DRAGON

Fay Sampson

Chris is always in trouble of one kind or another, but does try extra hard to be good when he is chosen to play Joseph in the school nativity play. This hilarious story ends with a glorious celebration of the Chinese New Year.